KID ★ AMAZING VS. THE BLOB

Josh Schneider

Clarion Books ★ Houghton Mifflin Harcourt ★ Boston New York

Clarion Books
3 Park Avenue
New York, New York 10016

Clarion Books is an imprint of Houghton Mifflin Harcourt Publishing Company.

www.hmhco.com

The illustrations in this book were done in watercolor and pen and ink.
The text was set in Arquitecta.

Library of Congress Cataloging-in-Publication Data is available.
ISBN 978-0-544-80125-7

Manufactured in China
SCP 10 9 8 7 6 5 4 3 2 1
4500646557

To Dana, for her daily superheroism.

AAAAAAAAAAA

ONE DAY, while practicing his letters, Jimmy is interrupted by an extremely annoying howl. And, right on cue, there's the emergency catastrophe alarm! Jimmy rushes to the closet. He touches the tennis racket like *this* and pulls the light string like *so* and—*whoosh!*—a secret door opens.

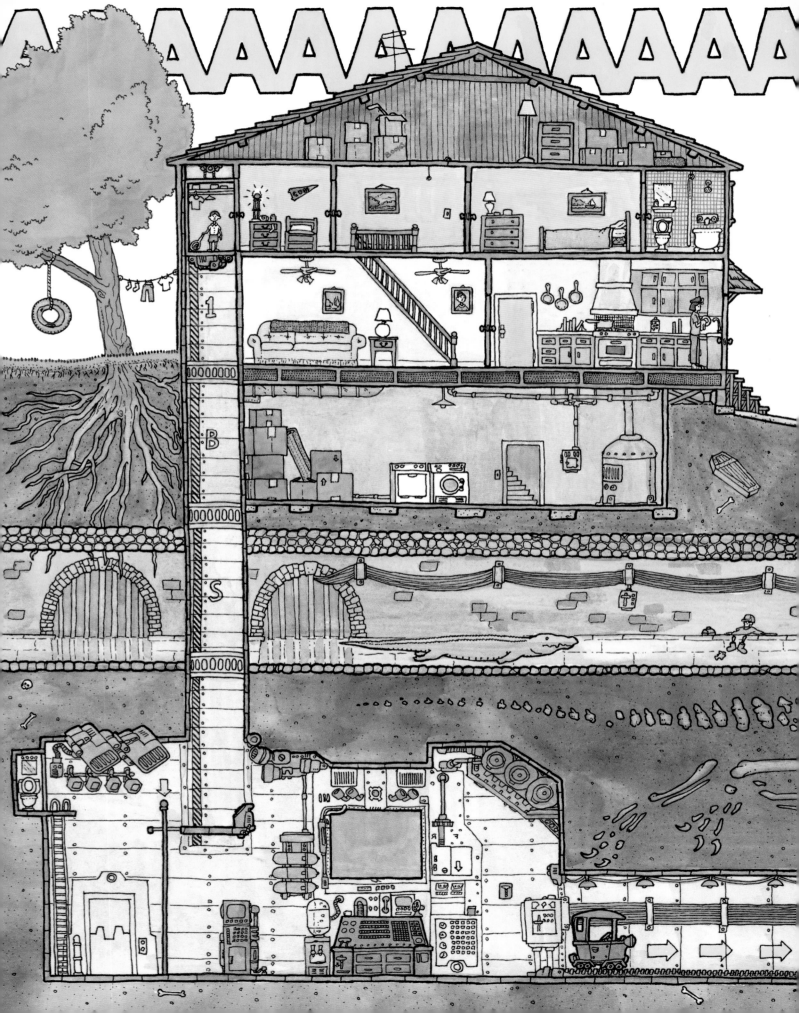

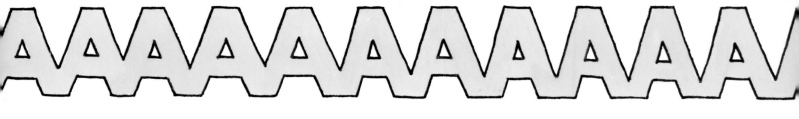

Jimmy goes through the secret door and into a secret elevator.
The secret elevator takes him down and down until he reaches a
secret base, where—

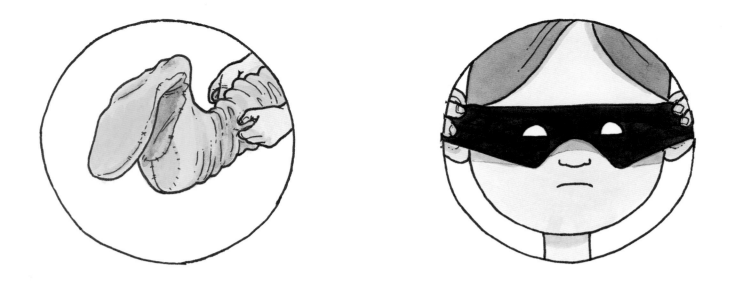

Kerzing! Jimmy is transformed into Kid Amazing!

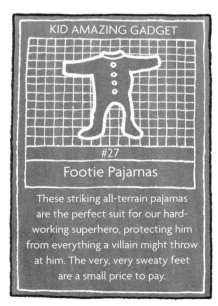

KID AMAZING GADGET

#27
Footie Pajamas

These striking all-terrain pajamas are the perfect suit for our hard-working superhero, protecting him from everything a villain might throw at him. The very, very sweaty feet are a small price to pay.

KID AMAZING GADGET

#55
Mystery Cloth

The origin of this mystery cloth is unknown (although it does bear a slight resemblance to a missing black tie). In any event, with the Kid's brilliant addition of two holes, it now keeps his secret identity safe.

KID AMAZING GADGET

#128

Dishwashing Gloves

When Kid Amazing rolls up his sleeves to take care of evil, these rare red dishwashing gloves are there to shield his mighty hands from lava, ice, lasers, acid, toxic goo, and pruny-ness.

KID AMAZING GADGET

#86

Baseball Cap

When duty calls, the cap of Jimmy, humble right fielder for Big Al's Automotive Little League team, becomes the cap of Kid Amazing, vanquisher of villainy and star pitcher for the Galactic Hero Little League team.

It's the Commissioner.

"What is it, Commissioner?" asks Kid Amazing.

"Jimmy—" says the Commissioner.

"Kid Amazing," says Kid Amazing.

"Kid Amazing," says the Commissioner. "Do you hear that howling? Could you please see what's going on?"

"I'm on it," says Kid Amazing. Who could it be?
An evil giant robot? Those space lobsters again?
No, only one thing could howl such an annoying howl:
Kid Amazing's arch-nemesis, the Blob!

"The Blob!" says Kid Amazing. "Don't worry. I'll take care of *her.*"

Kid Amazing uses his robo-sniffer to catch the Blob's terrible scent. The stink trail leads right to the Blob's lair.

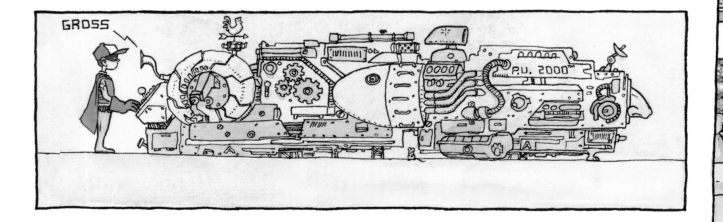

Kid Amazing opens the door and leaps back.

It's the Blob's terrible stink cloud!

It smells worse than ten thousand rotten melons.

It smells worse than one million warthogs.

It smells worse than *cat food.*

It is probably the worst thing ever.

Kid Amazing quick-thinkingly grabs his de-stinking spray from his utility belt, and—*spritz!* So much for *that* stink cloud.

Entering the Blob's lair,
Kid Amazing slips and slides
on the slime-covered floor.

The Blob must be close.

But to reach her, he must clear a safe, slip-free path. Kid Amazing reaches for his de-sliming wipe and—*fwip!*—the lair is dry.

KID AMAZING GADGET

#381

Clown-Print Scarf

Another of the Commisioner's mysteriously unused birthday presents, now a stylish and absorbent scourge of evildoers everywhere.

And there on her throne is the Blob.

She is howling a terrible, annoying howl.

Kid Amazing reaches for his utility belt, but it's empty!

He is out of de-stinking spray.

He is out of de-sliming wipes.

What will Kid Amazing do?

The howl is melting his brain. He dives for cover.

Then he sees it: the Blob's howl neutralizer.

Kid Amazing grabs the neutralizer and—*pop!*—the Blob stops howling.

POP!

Kid Amazing has saved the day.

"I have saved the day," says Kid Amazing. "Also, the Blob needs a new stink-containment unit."

"Thanks," says the Commissioner. "But please stop calling your sister the Blob."

"No thanks necessary," says Kid Amazing. "Saving the day is its own reward. Although a cookie is also a very good reward."

"I'll see what I can do," says the Commissioner.

"Another happy ending for the forces of justice," says Kid Amazing.
"That's the last trouble we'll get from *her.*"